Katie and the Bathers

JAMES MAYHEW

ORCHARD

For Little Katie Light

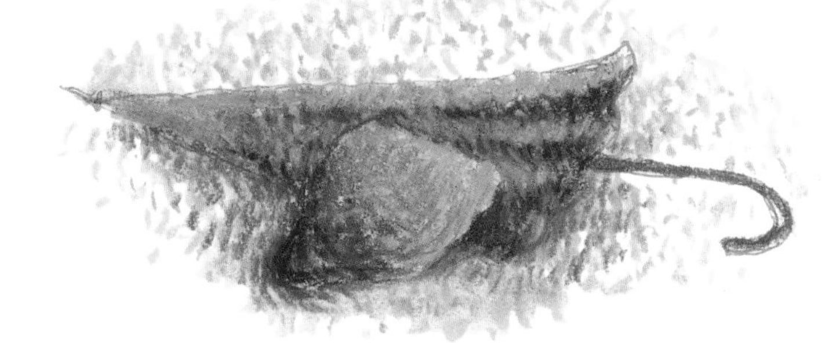

and for Vanessa Hadfield and Liz Johnson (I couldn't have done it without you!)

ORCHARD BOOKS
338 Euston Road, London NW1 3BH
Orchard Books Australia
Level 17/207 Kent Street, Sydney, NSW 2000

ISBN 978 1 40833 189 7

First published in 2004 by Orchard Books
First published in paperback in 2005
This edition published in 2015

A CIP catalogue record for this book is available from the British Library.

1 3 5 7 9 10 8 6 4 2

Printed in China

Orchard Books is an imprint of Hachette Children's Group and published by The Watts Publishing Group Limited, an Hachette UK company.
www.hachette.co.uk

www.jamesmayhew.co.uk

Acknowledgements
Bathers at Asnières, 1884 (oil on canvas), Seurat, Georges Pierre (1859-91) / National Gallery, London, UK / Bridgeman Images. *Sunday Afternoon on the Island of La Grande Jatte*, 1884-86 (oil on canvas), Seurat, Georges Pierre (1859-91) / The Art Institute of Chicago, IL, USA / Bridgeman Images. *Port of Honfleur*, c.1886 (oil on canvas), Seurat, Georges Pierre (1859-91) / The Barnes Foundation, Philadelphia, Pennsylvania, USA / Bridgeman Images. *Woman Hanging up the Washing*, 1887 (oil on canvas), Pissarro, Camille (1830-1903) / Musee d'Orsay, Paris, France / Bridgeman Images. *Portrait of Felix Feneon in 1890* (oil on canvas), Signac, Paul (1863-1935) / Museum of Modern Art, New York, USA / Bridgeman Images.

IT WAS A SUNNY DAY, and Katie and Grandma were feeling hot and bothered.

"Let's go swimming," said Grandma. "I'll get our swimsuits."

When they got to the pool,
it was already full.
"Never mind, we'll come back later,"
said Grandma. "The art gallery is
nearby. Let's go there for a while."

In the gallery, it felt even hotter! While Grandma had a little snooze, Katie found a room full of amazing pictures. They were painted in thousands of brightly coloured dots.

Katie saw a painting called *Bathers at Asnières* by Georges Seurat. She could almost feel the breeze blowing over the soft grass and hear the gurgling river.

"What a great place for a swim!" thought Katie, so she climbed over the frame and inside the picture.

It was warm and peaceful in the picture – the sun shone, oars splashed and a boy in a red hat called to the boats racing on the river. Katie saw a little bathing hut and decided to change into her swimsuit . . .

. . . then she jumped into the water with an enormous splash!

"*Bonjour*!" said the boy in the red hat. "I'm Jacques."

"I'm Katie," said Katie. "Isn't this lovely?"

"*Oui*!" laughed Jacques. "*Très bon*!"

After lots more splashing, Katie sat down on the picture frame to rest. But it started to tip . . .

. . . and the river began pouring into the gallery!

"This is better than the swimming pool!" Katie laughed.

But then they heard a sigh from another painting by Seurat called *Sunday Afternoon on the Island of La Grande Jatte.* Katie saw a little girl in a white dress. She looked rather sad, so Katie climbed inside the picture.

Katie found herself in a park where everyone looked very elegant and grand.
"Oh, you are lucky," sighed the little girl. "It's such a hot day but no one is allowed to bathe in this painting."

"Come and paddle in the gallery!" said Katie. "It's lovely and cool."
"Oh Prudence, please say yes!" pleaded the girl to her governess.
"Well, be sure to keep your clothes dry, Josette," said Prudence.

“What a splendid idea!” said the elegant people. “Let’s paddle too!” The ladies hitched up their skirts and the gentlemen rolled up their trousers, and then they all had a wonderful time paddling in the gallery.

But water was still pouring out of the painting . . .
“It’s getting too deep to paddle,” said Josette,
standing on the steps.
“How will we get back over to our picture?”
said the elegant people. “We can’t
swim in these clothes!”

"Let's fetch a boat!" said Katie. She pointed to another picture by Seurat, called *Port of Honfleur.* Katie and Jacques swam over to the painting and quickly clambered inside.

They found a little rowing boat in the harbour.
It was quite heavy but they managed to drag
it over the frame and into the gallery.
Then off they rowed to the rescue!

"We'll go first!" said Prudence,
helping Josette into the boat.
But when it was her turn,
her foot slipped, the boat
moved away and . . .

SPLASH!

Prudence fell into the water!
"Just look at my dress!" she wailed.
"How will I ever get dry?"

“Perhaps she’ll help,” said Katie, pointing to a picture called *Woman Hanging up the Washing* by Camille Pissarro. Prudence scrambled inside the painting, followed by Katie and Josette, while Jacques rowed off to rescue the elegant people and take them back to their picture.

The kindly washerwoman gave Prudence some clothes to wear and hung out her wet dress to dry. Then Katie, Josette and the washerwoman's daughter played in the sun as the women chatted.

Suddenly, Katie heard Jacques calling from the boat.
"We must get back to our pictures," said Jacques. "The guard is coming!"
"The guard!" gasped Katie. "He'll be horrified when he sees all this water!"

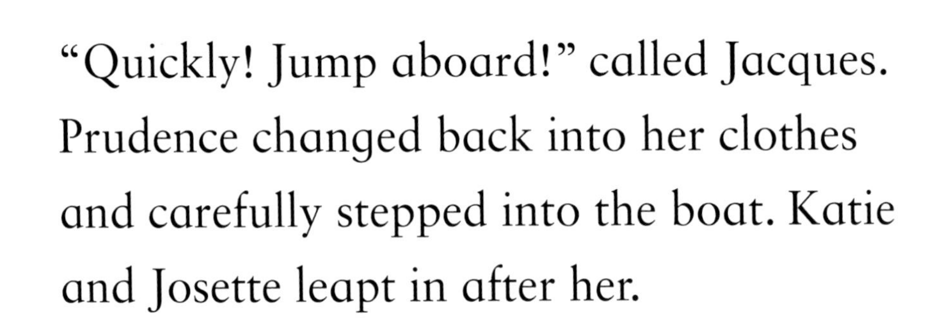

"Quickly! Jump aboard!" called Jacques. Prudence changed back into her clothes and carefully stepped into the boat. Katie and Josette leapt in after her.

Jacques rowed across the gallery while Katie desperately tried to think of a way to get rid of the water. They passed all sorts of pictures; none of them looked very useful. Then Katie saw a painting by Paul Signac called *Portrait of Felix Feneon.*

"He looks like a magician," said Katie, so she called, "Excuse me, can you do any magic? The gallery is a mess and the guard is coming!"

Felix wanted to help, so he leant out of the painting, waved his stick over his hat and shouted, "ABRACADABRA!" Coloured swirls came out of his picture, but the gallery was still flooded.
"I'll try again," he said. "ALLA-KAZAM!"

"Oh dear," said Felix, as stars and rainbows floated into the gallery. "I'm not very good at magic."

Just then, they all heard footsteps. It was the guard!
"Oh, please try once more!" begged Katie.
"ALLA-KAZOOM! Clear up this room!" said Felix.

There was a flash of light and everything vanished in a swirl of stars and colours. Katie found she was standing in her dry clothes and everyone and everything was back where it belonged – just in time!

The guard looked carefully around the room.
Everything was exactly as it should be.
"Thank you everyone," whispered Katie.
"I've had a wonderful time!"

As soon as the guard had gone, Katie gently woke Grandma.
"Would you like to go swimming now?" yawned Grandma.
"I don't feel quite so hot any more!" laughed Katie.
"In that case, you won't be wanting an ice cream either," said Grandma.
"Oh, I can always manage an ice cream," said Katie.
"Me too!" smiled Grandma. And off they went.

Get creative with Katie!

Georges Seurat invented an exciting new way of painting called Pointillism. The pictures are made up of dots of carefully chosen colour. You can create your own Pointillist pictures, too! Try dipping the hard end of a paint-brush into the paint to make dots on paper, or just use your fingers! I've used mine to make a picture of a boat. I got a bit messy, but I had lots of fun. I bet you will too!

Love Katie!x